FROGGY'S HALLOWEEN

FROGGY'S HALLOWEEN

by JONATHAN LONDON
illustrated by FRANK REMKIEWICZ

PUFFIN BOOKS

For Froggy's spooky Uncle Rod & scary Auntie Ann with thanks to crazy Marilynne, librarian fatale
    —J. L.

For John and Elise, who also dress funny
    —F. R.

PUFFIN BOOKS
Published by the Penguin Group
Penguin Putnam Books for Young Readers, 345 Hudson Street, New York, New York 10014, U.S.A.
Penguin Books Ltd, 27 Wrights Lane, London W8 5TZ, England
Penguin Books Australia Ltd, Ringwood, Victoria, Australia
Penguin Books Canada Ltd, 10 Alcorn Avenue, Toronto, Ontario, Canada M4V 3B2
Penguin Books (N.Z.) Ltd, 182-190 Wairau Road, Auckland 10, New Zealand

Penguin Books Ltd, Registered Offices: Harmondsworth, Middlesex, England

First published in the United States of America by Viking,
a member of Penguin Putnam Books for Young Readers, 1999
Published by Puffin Books, a division of Penguin Putnam Books for Young Readers, 2001

23 25 27 29 30 28 26 24

THE LIBRARY OF CONGRESS HAS CATALOGED THE VIKING EDITION AS FOLLOWS:
London, Jonathan, date
Froggy's Halloween / by Jonathan London ; illustrated by Frank Remkiewicz
p. cm.
Summary: Froggy tries to find just the right costume for Halloween, and although
his trick-or-treating does not go as he had planned, he enjoys himself anyway.
ISBN 0-670-88449-9 (hardcover)
[1. Halloween—Fiction. 2. Frogs—Fiction.] I. Remkiewicz, Frank, ill. II. Title.
PZ7.L8432Fv 1999 [E]—dc21 98-47720 CIP AC

Puffin Books ISBN 978-0-14-230068-8

Printed in the United States of America
Set in Kabel

For Froggy, Halloween
meant candy.
But it also meant dressing up.
And he wondered,
"What should I be for Halloween?"

"I know!" cried Froggy.
"Super Frog!"

"Flying high over the city.
Faster than a dragonfly!
Stronger than a bullfrog!"

No. Something spooky.
"I know!" cried Froggy.
"Ghost Frog!"

He poked two holes
in his mother's best white sheet
and draped it over his head—

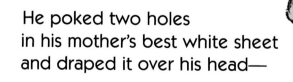

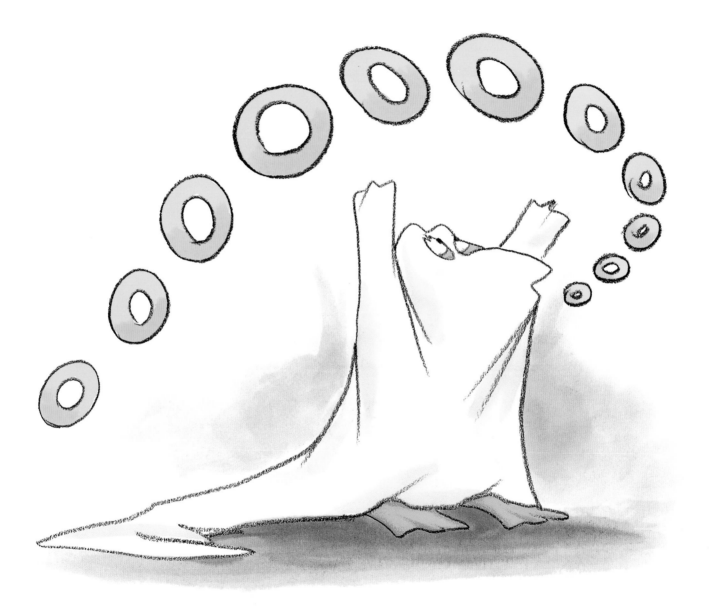

No. Something scarier.
"I know!" cried Froggy.
"Vampire Frog!"
He put on his black cape—*zwoosh!*
Pulled on his mom's black tights—*zup!*

Put on his slick black wig—*zat!*

And said in his best Dracula voice:
"Trrrick or trrreat, smell my feet.
Give me something good to eat.

If you don't, I don't care—
I'll pull down your *undervear*!"

FRRROOGGYY !

called his mother.

"Wha-a-a-t?"

"Halloween's not till next week! You're supposed to be doing your homework, dear!"

"I'm Count Von Frogula," said Froggy. "Vampire frogs don't *do* homeverk!"

Froggy's mother laughed.
"Vampires have *fangs!*" she said.
"You're a toothless wonder!"
"Oops!" cried Froggy, covering his mouth.

So all week at school, Froggy wondered,
"What should I be for Halloween?"
A football player?
A cowboy?
A zombie?

FRRROOGGYY!

cried his teacher, Miss Witherspoon.

"Wha-a-a-t?"

"Kindly keep your mind on your work, dear."

But his mind was on Halloween.
Every day after school he got ready.
He carved crazy pumpkins.
He hung sticky spiderwebs
all over the front of his house.
He hung his mother's sheet
like a ghost in the wind.
And he practiced:
"Trick or treat, smell my feet.
Give me something good to eat.
If you don't, I don't care—
I'll pull down your *underwear*!"

At last, it was the night before Halloween.
And all through the house
there were *cre-e-e-e-a-king* sounds
and *scra-a-a-a-tching* sounds.
Froggy was scared.
He shivered in bed
and imagined ghosts and goblins
and werewolves and witches.
Witches! *Zap!*
"I know!" cried Froggy.
"I'll be the Frog Prince for
Halloween!"

And in the morning,
he put on his black cape—*zwoosh!*
Pulled on his mom's black tights—*zup!*

Put on his slick black wig —*zat!*

Plunked on a gold crown—*zunk!*

And flashed
his mighty sword—"*ta-da-a-a!*"

At the Halloween parade at school,
all the girls thought he looked cute—
especially Frogilina.

And that night, when the dark crept in,
and all the ghosts and goblins
crept out to trick-or-treat— BOO!

Princess Frogilina leapt out
and chased after the Frog Prince
to give him a kiss!

EEEEEEEEEEEK !

cried Froggy.
He was never more scared in his life!

He leapfrogged over his mother.
He leapfrogged over his father.
He leapfrogged over his friend Max
and flopped up Max's steps—
flop flop . . . splat!
He tripped on the porch—

and Frogilina fell on top of him!

The door flew open and—*uh-oh*—
there stood the wickedest witch in the world.
"Trick-or-treat?" squeaked Froggy,
looking more red in the face than green.

Luckily, Frogilina ran away
and the witch turned out to be Max's granny.
And that Halloween
Froggy got tons of candy.
But his sword had torn a hole
in his candy bag.
And by the time he got home . . .

his candy was *all gone*.
"Oh no!" cried Froggy.
"What's the matter?" asked his mother.
He showed her his empty bag.

"Well you're in luck," said his mother, holding up a full bowl.
"I guess nobody liked my treats."
And what do you think she gave him?
Chocolate-covered . . .

flies!
"Yum!" cried Froggy. "My favorite!"—
munch crunch munch.